USE THESE EGGSQUISITE STICKERS TO DECORATE YOUR OWN EGGS!

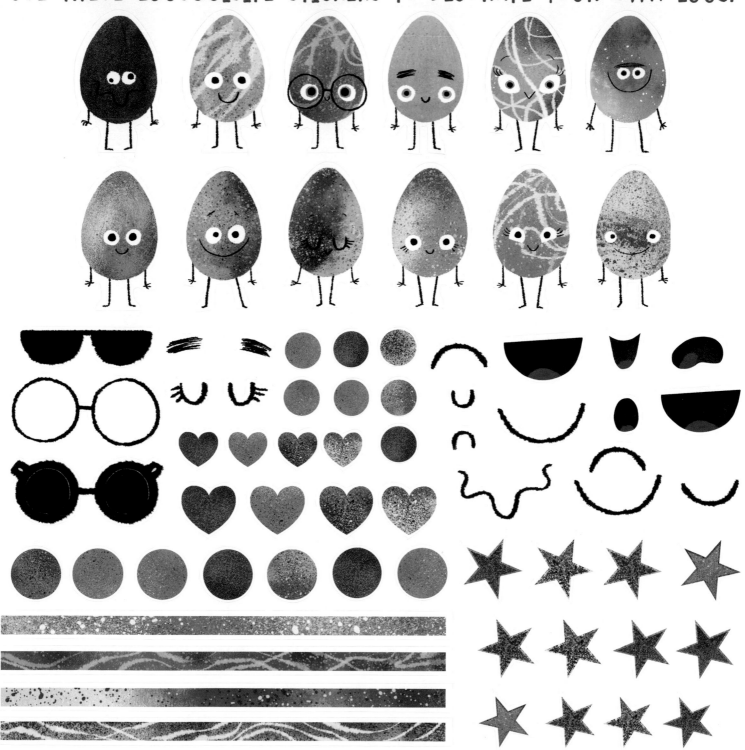

HARPER
An Imprint of HarperCollinsPublishers

THE GREAT EGGSCAPE!

Written by **Jory John** • Cover illustration by **Pete Oswald**

Interior illustrations by **Saba Joshaghani** based on artwork by Pete Oswald

HARPER

An Imprint of HarperCollinsPublishers

ISBN 978-0-06-297567-6

The artist used pencil sketches scanned and painted in
Adobe Photoshop to create the digital illustrations
for this book.

21 22 23 RTLO 10 9 8 7 6 5
❖
First Edition

HOWDY.

I'm Shel. An egg.
How's it going?

It's just me today. I'm on my own.
The other eggs? Where are they?
Good question.

The thing is . . . sometimes they leave the carton on weekends, before the customers arrive. They escape into the store.

They call it:

"THE GREAT EGGSCAPE!"

LOCAL FARM FRESH EGGS

LOCAL FARM FRESH EGGS

(Escape . . . eggscape . . . you get it.)

Me? I'm not really in the mood to run around, if you want to know the truth. I'd rather just sit here. I don't mind a little "me time."

No reason to go frolic with everybody else. I prefer adventures of the imagination.
It's quite peaceful here, without all the other eggs.

Sure, there's a part of me that wonders what they're doing, right this very moment.

I have a few guesses.

RIGHT THIS VERY MOMENT . . .

We look amazing!

So festive!

Let's play a game!

Ahhhhhh. This is the life.

When you live in a carton with a lot of roommates, you never get much peace and quiet.

So I'm going to enjoy this while it lasts.

Exactly two hours, thirty-six minutes, and two seconds later ...

Hmm. Nobody's back yet?
Where are Clegg and Meg and Peg
and Egbert and Greg and Shelby
and Shelly and Sheldon and Frank
and Other Frank? Did I forget
anybody?
Anyway, they should've been
home by now.

These Great Eggscapes are usually over by lunch,
when everybody gets hungry.

I'll just wait a few more minutes.
They'll surely be home quite soon.

No reason to stress.

No reason to pace.

No reason to get all worked up.

BONG!

Noon? **IT'S NOON!**
Morning is officially OVER.

OK, now I'm getting nervous.

Where are my friends?

Are they OK?

Should I go
look for them?

But what if they come
home while I'm away?

I JUST DON'T KNOW WHAT TO DO!

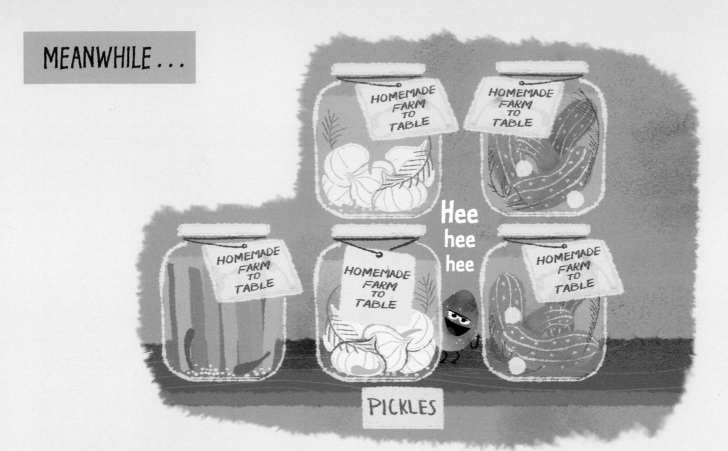

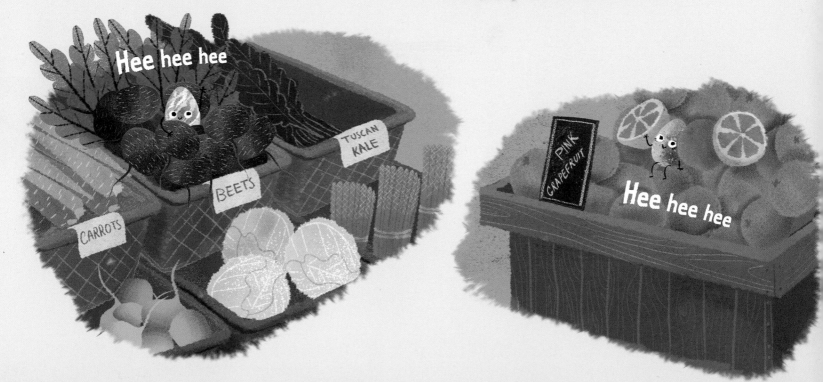

I must find them! Where do I start?
Maybe in aisle 1. That seems promising.

Pickles,

pickles,

pickles,

it's all PICKLES.
Sheesh!

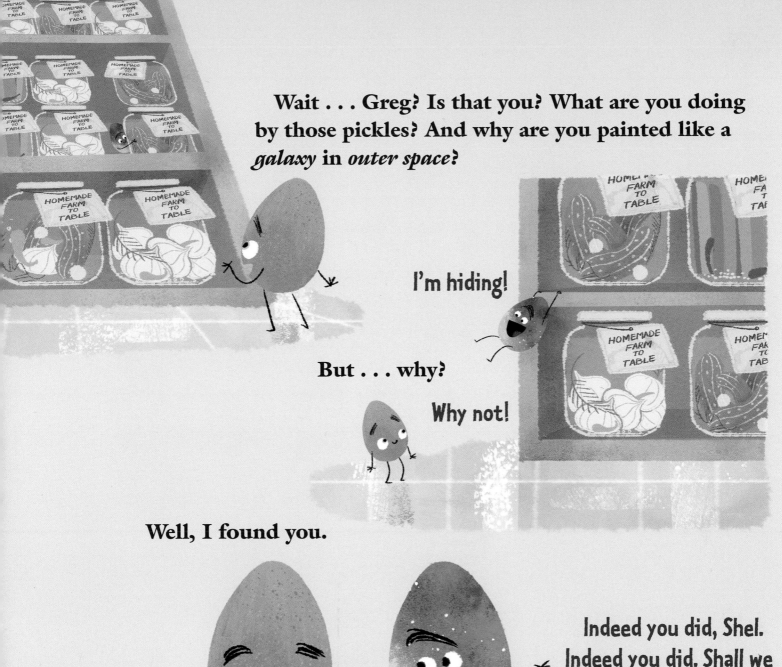

Found you,

found you,

BEETS

there you are,

found you.

Is that everybody? Line up, eggs! Let's see, we have you and you and you and you and you and you and you and you and you and *you*. That's ten eggs, plus me, which equals eleven. Hmm.

WAIT JUST A MINUTE. . . . .

Where's Meg?

Has anybody seen Meg?

MEEEGGG!

Wait, where are you guys going?

To get some lunch, Shel. Then maybe take a nap.

Hide-and-seek is tiring.

Meg will turn up eventually. She always does.

EGGS! HALT! As the old saying goes, "If a fellow egg is hiding, we must look until we find them."

Or maybe that's a new saying. Anyway, we're not finished until we're all back together as a dozen. Got it?

GOOD! LET'S GO!

Greg, search the high shelves! Peg, check the low shelves! Clegg, don't forget the middle shelves! Sheldon, look through that bag of marshmallows! Shelby, comb aisle 5! Egbert, investigate aisle 6! Me? I'll scour the discount aisle! Meg has got to be around here somewhere!

Shell! Shell! I found a note by the cash register. It might be a clue!

WELL, READ IT, GREG!

OK, OK, you don't have to yell.

"If you want to find an egg,
Just like a pot of gold,
Go where things are sold in bulk,
And look for something bold."

It *was* a clue, Shell! I mean, it *is* a clue!

Indeed, Greg. Indeed.

Hmm. Bulk . . .

bold . . . bulk . . .

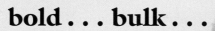

bold . . . bulk . . .

Wait . . . I think I've got it!

Wow, there are just so many bins. But which one is the right one? How would we know?

Um, Shel, remember how the clue said to look for something bold? Do you think Meg is hiding in there?

Of course, Peg!

OF COURSE!

EGGS!
SHOULDER STACK!
UNITE!
Hee hee hee
BOLD COFFEE
COLOMBIAN COFFEE
Knock knock, we know you're in there, Meg!

Oh, hi. I thought you were never going to find me. Nice work, Shel. Glad you found your way out of the carton, for once, and into the world.

Thanks, Meg, but it wasn't just me. We found you as a group. And now we're back together again.
Whew!

You know . . . looking for eggs is fun.
Finding eggs is more fun.

But the most fun of all?

WITH YOUR FRIENDS.

Say, when's the next Great Eggscape?
Shall we do this again tomorrow?

Indeed we shall, Shel.